P9-DFX-432

Sam McBratney

There, There

ILLUSTRATED BY

Ivan Bates

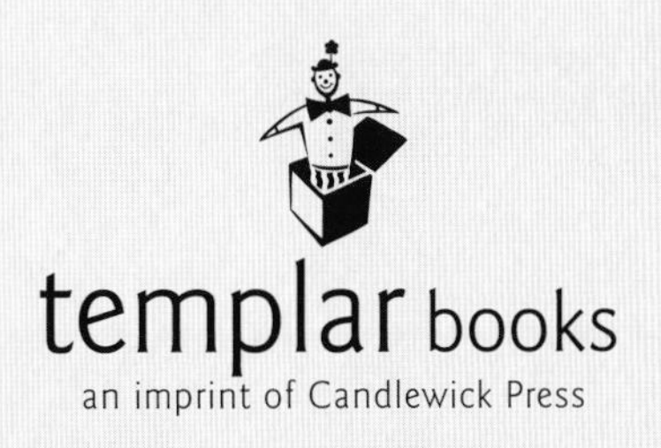

templar books
an imprint of Candlewick Press

Little Hansie Bear,
who loved to pretend,
thought it would be fun
to walk like a duck.

Unfortunately he fell
over sideways into
a deep-down ditch.
He hurt his knee and
couldn't get out again.

His dad came to help.
"What were you doing?" he asked.
"I was trying to walk like a duck!"

"Well, that's not easy," said
Hansie's dad, "unless you *are* a duck.
Let's put a bandage on that knee."
He gave Hansie a big hug.
"There, there, it won't be sore
for long—you'll see."

And he was right.
After a few minutes
and a few jumps,

just to be sure . . .
Hansie was ready
to play again.

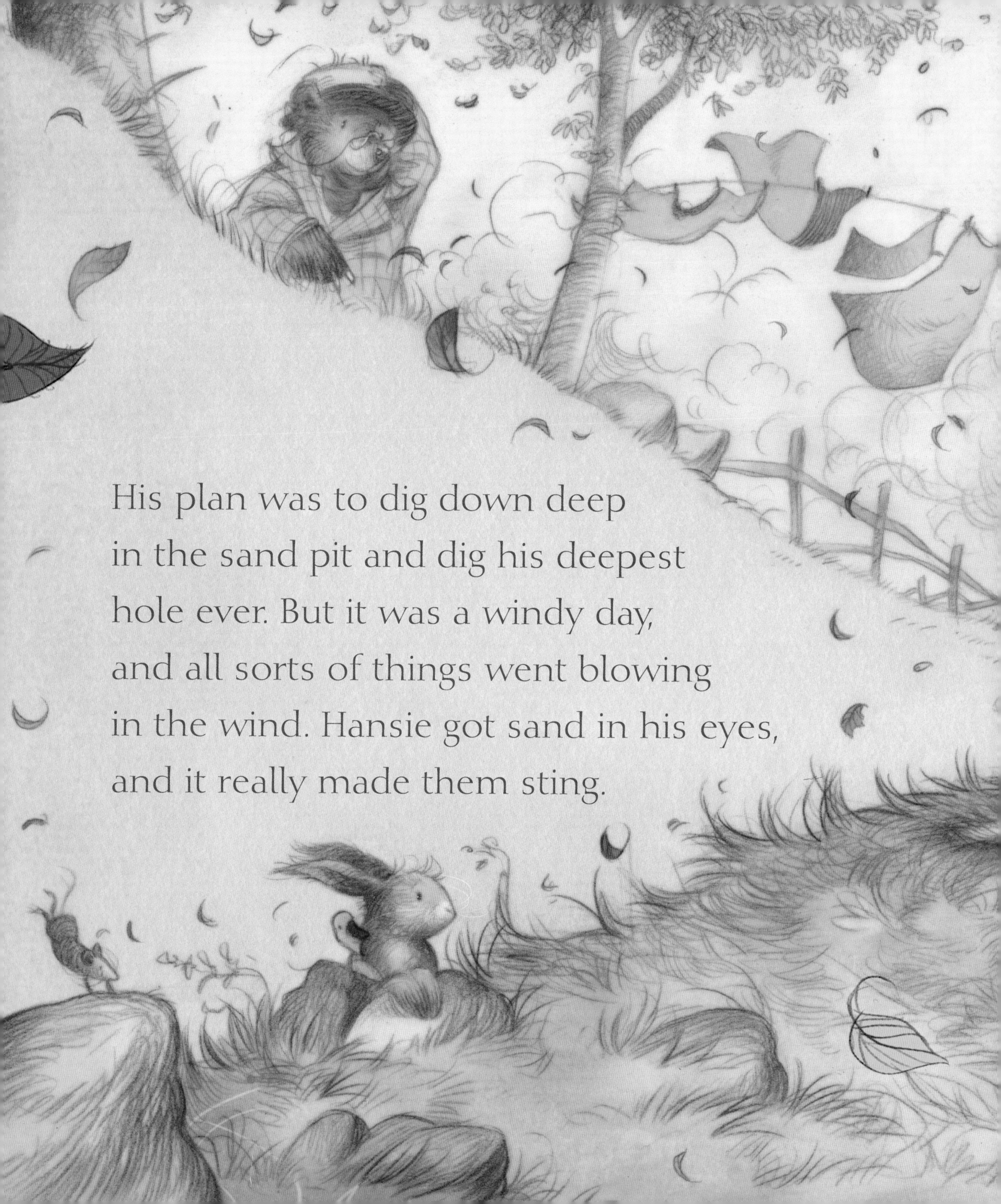

His plan was to dig down deep
in the sand pit and dig his deepest
hole ever. But it was a windy day,
and all sorts of things went blowing
in the wind. Hansie got sand in his eyes,
and it really made them sting.

His dad, who was still close by,
picked him up for a cuddle.
"There, there," he said.
"Do blinkety-blink like this,
and you'll soon be better."

Hansie blinked his eyes . . .
then a few more blinks
just to be sure . . .
and his eyes were as
good as ever.

Then some of
Hansie's friends
came to play
on his swing in
the tree . . .

but guess what!

Hansie bumped his
head on a branch, and
it was a hard bump.

Dad saw what happened.
"There, there, Hansie," he said.
"I'll give it a rub, and
you'll be fine."

And he was right again.

Hansie Bear ran off
to play a game
of hide-and-seek
with his friends.

Later that same afternoon, when
the friends had all gone home,
Hansie saw his father coming
very slowly through the gate.

Hansie ran to meet him.

"I hurt my foot," said Dad. "I stepped on a thorn, and my goodness it is sore!"

"Were you trying to walk like a duck?"

"I was *not* trying to walk like a duck."

Soon Mom came to see what was happening.
They made Dad sit on the garden seat.
"Ouch!" he said as Mom pulled out the thorn.
"We are *definitely* not having a good day!"

This is like falling into the deep-down ditch.
Or getting sand in your eyes.
Or bumping your head a hard bump.

"*I* know
a good thing to do!"
said Hansie. . . .

And he gave his dad one
of his tightest hugs ever.
And then Hansie said,

"There, there, we'll be
all right now."

And so they were.

For Caroline
To mark a fine collaboration
S. McB.

For Rachel,
with love
I. B.

Produced by Brubaker, Ford & Friends

First U.S. edition 2013

Library of Congress Catalog Card Number 2012954336
ISBN 978-0-7636-6702-3

13 14 15 16 17 18 TLF 10 9 8 7 6 5 4 3 2 1

Printed in Dongguan, Guangdong, China

This book was typeset in Diotima Roman, Goudy Bold, and Times Bold.
The illustrations were done in mixed media.

TEMPLAR BOOKS

an imprint of
Candlewick Press
99 Dover Street
Somerville, Massachusetts 02144
www.candlewick.com